GN00870314

Dedicated to

My three beautiful sons

Niko, Taro, and Kyno

From little boys to fine young men
Your encouragement and belief in me made this possible
I love you to the moon and back always.

Special mention to Willow, Daisy, Arum, Cataleya, Oliva, Will, Joshua, Henry, Ethan, Mia, Olly, Jude, Remi, Alfie, Charlie, and Summer. Not forgetting the newest family member, one very special boy, my Godson Jasper. Happy sleeping and sleep well.

Thank you to my husband, Cliff, for your patience, Carli Fish, for all your help and advice. Luke, for your feedback, Megan Ayers, for proofreading, Manuel Garfio, for formatting and TullipStudios for making this story come alive with your wonderful illustrations.

Copyright 2019 © by Anna Rowe

Illustrations by Tulip Studios 2019

ISBN 978-0-9568327-9-5

First published as an audio CD by Anna Rowe of Natural Harmony Productions Ltd 2010 © & (p)

Published by Anna Rowe Natural Harmony Productions Ltd www.naturalharmonyproductions.com

Note to the reader

Twinkle and the Magic Carpet is a wonderful addition to a bedtime routine. This is a story to aid your child to fall asleep. As with all books, your little one will want to familiarise themselves with the characters in the book. This will help them to feel comfortable with the story and make it easier for them to relax, ready for sleep. For best results, we recommend that your child is lying down while listening to you read the story to them.

Using the reading instructions below will aid the best results.

Throughout the story, you will see

~ ..... (five dots), this is a sign for you to pause between words.

~ *Italic text* indicates that it is time for you to use your most gentle, soft and calm, voice.

This book contains specially constructed relaxation sentences. These will guide your child's unconscious mind to relax and fall asleep.

It is our aim that your little one will fall asleep, but we give no guarantee to this outcome.

Attention reader – This is a story that encourages sleep. Do not read out loud next to a person driving a car or operating machinery that requires wakefulness.

Twinkle &
the Magic Carpet

Sleep sleep sleep now....

Twinkle and the Magic Carpet
Sleep sleep sleep now...

Snuggle down into bed now (child's name/special name)

Wriggle your body to make yourself comfortable .....

Feel the covers making you cosy and warm ..... so cosy and warm .....

Once upon a time, there was a little girl called Georgie. Now whenever Georgie wanted to sleep she would imagine that she was on a soft, cosy magic carpet. One night, she imagined that she was looking out of her window, up at the stars, and all of a sudden, a little star up above in the sky so high started to *float down to earth .....*

All the way down ..... Now Georgie knew her nursery rhymes and knew that this was Twinkle twinkle little star, she knew that she had to save Twinkle as Twinkle was like a diamond in the sky.

People would not notice Twinkle during the day when the sun was out as

Twinkle would be asleep, but when night came, everyone welcomed

Twinkle's little light that would shine, all through the night.

Georgie snuggled into her soft, cosy, magic carpet and said the magic words

three times ..... *sleep* ..... *sleep* ..... *sleep* ..... Now Georgie told the

magic carpet that they needed to save Twinkle twinkle little star and to get

Twinkle back in the sky because the travellers in the dark would look for

Twinkle's tiny spark to light the way at night .....

As Georgie said the magic words ..... *sleep* ..... *sleep* ..... *sleep* ..... the magic carpet started to glow and then *gently* ..... *ever so gently* ..... it *started to float across the sky* in search of Twinkle. As they drifted through, the sky fluffy white clouds came floating by. Georgie stopped and asked the fluffy white clouds if they had seen Twinkle twinkle little star. They replied they had seen Twinkle *floating down* ..... *down* through some trees, not far from where they were. But they couldn't help Twinkle as they needed to stay in the sky because without Twinkle's light they couldn't travel at night. Georgie thanked the fluffy white clouds and told them that she would do her best to find and help Twinkle to get back in the sky. The fluffy white clouds thanked Georgie and said, "Goodbye."

Georgie and the magic carpet looked down below at the rooftops of the

houses and homes nearby but couldn't see Twinkle ..... Then they floated

over the fields and farms ..... But still, Twinkle was nowhere to be

seen, "Where could twinkle be?"

Then ..... there at the top of a tree sat a beautiful, wise old owl .....

Georgie stopped and asked the wise old owl if he had seen

Twinkle twinkle little star? ..... Owl replied he had seen Twinkle

floating down ..... down through some trees ..... not far from

where they were but couldn't help Twinkle as he was stuck,

because without Twinkle's light he couldn't travel at night .....

Georgie thanked the wise old owl and told him that she would do

her best to find and help Twinkle to get back in the sky.

The wise old owl thanked Georgie and said ..... "Goodbye."

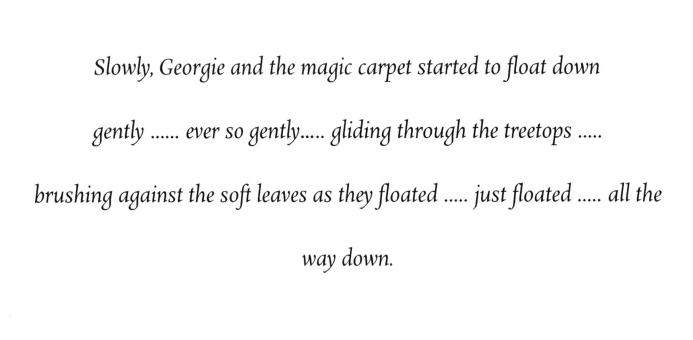

Slowly, Georgie and the magic carpet started to float down

gently ...... ever so gently..... gliding through the treetops .....

brushing against the soft leaves as they floated ..... just floated ..... all the

way down.

There they met Mummy Fox. Georgie stopped and asked

Mummy Fox if she had seen Twinkle twinkle little star.

Mummy Fox replied she had seen Twinkle *floating down* .....

down through some trees ..... not far from where they were,

but couldn't help Twinkle as she was lost, because without

Twinkle's light she couldn't travel at night ..... Georgie thanked

Mummy Fox and told her that she would do her best to find and

help Twinkle to get back in the sky. The Mummy Fox

thanked Georgia and said ..... "Goodbye."

Georgie and the magic carpet glided gently above the ground and

suddenly heard a rustling sound and there they saw

Mr. Bunny Rabbit poking his head out of a hole. Georgia stopped

and asked Mr. Bunny Rabbit if he had seen Twinkle twinkle little

star, Mr. Bunny Rabbit told Georgie that he had not seen

Twinkle because he had been pushing and pushing at his front

door, and do you know ..... it would not move! So then he had to

come out of his back door .....

Mr. Bunny Rabbit asked Georgie if she would help to find his front door, because without Twinkle's light he could not see at night ..... Georgie told Mr. Bunny Rabbit to hop on her magic carpet and she would help him to find his front door.

They slowly glided above the ground, and then they noticed a tiny flickering light ..... and there on the top of Mr. Bunny Rabbit's front door ..... nestled in some leaves, lay Twinkle twinkle little star ..... fast asleep ......

The magic carpet gently lowered to the ground.

Georgie and Mr. Bunny Rabbit tried very hard not to make a sound

but Twinkle woke up, looked at

Georgie and Mr. Bunny Rabbit and asked, "Where am I?"

Mr. Bunny Rabbit told Twinkle that, "You're on top of my front door

and without your light, I cannot see at night."

Twinkle told them, "I should be in the sky, lighting the way for all the

travellers passing by, I must have fallen asleep!

Oh my ... I should be in the sky."

Georgie told Twinkle not to worry as they could travel on her

magic carpet, and magic carpet would take Twinkle back up high,

where Twinkle can shine like a diamond in the sky.

Georgie and Twinkle snuggled into her soft, cosy magic carpet and

said the magic words three times

..... *sleep* ..... *sleep* ..... *sleep* .....

The magic carpet started to glow and then gently ..... ever

so gently ..... it started to float ..... they said, "Night, night"

to Mr. Bunny Rabbit.

Mr. Bunny Rabbit was happy now he had found his front door

he thanked them and said,

"Goodnight."

As the magic carpet floated some more, they saw Mummy Fox on

the forest floor. They said, "Night, night," to Mummy Fox,

Mummy Fox was happy because with Twinkle's light she could

now travel at night. She thanked them and said,

"Goodnight."

The magic carpet floated up through the trees, gently brushing

against the soft leaves and there at the top of the tree sat the wise

old owl ..... They said, "Night, night," to wise old owl .....

Owl, was happy because with Twinkle's light he could now travel

at night ..... He thanked them and said,

"Goodnight."

Upwards they floated until they reached the fluffy, white clouds

floating by. They said, "Night, night," to the fluffy, white clouds.

The fluffy, white clouds were happy because with

Twinkle's light, they could now travel at night.

They thanked them and said,

"Goodnight."

Georgie and the magic carpet continued to float and drift up high

so they could put Twinkle back in the sky. When they reached

the highest point, Twinkle's light became so bright.

Twinkle started floating off the carpet into the night.

Twinkle was so happy now and told them, ...

"For in the dark blue skies I keep, I promise never to

shut my eyes, and sleep, till the sun is in the sky."

Twinkle thanked Georgie and the magic carpet and said,

"Bye, bye."

Georgie snuggled into her soft, cosy magic carpet and again said

the magic words three times,

sleep ..... sleep ..... sleep ..... Now the magic carpet started to

glow and then gently ..... ever so gently ..... It started to float

down ..... all the way down ..... for Georgia to sleep ..... with a

lovely rhyme for her to keep.

Twinkle, twinkle, little star,
How I wonder what you are!
Up above the world so high,
Like a diamond in the sky!

When the blazing sun is gone,
When there's nothing to shine upon,
Then you show your little light,
Twinkle, twinkle, all the night.

Then the traveller in the dark,
Thank you for your tiny spark,
He could not see which way to go,
If you did not twinkle so.

In the dark blue sky, you keep,
And often through my curtains peep,
For you never shut your eye,
Till the sun is in the sky.

As your bright and tiny spark,
Lights the traveller in the dark,
Though I know not what you are,
Twinkle, twinkle, little star.

Night, night ..... Shhh ..... shhh ..... shhh

About the Author:

Anna Rowe is a therapist and certified practitioner of Neurological Repatterning. She created the 'Sleep, sleep, sleep ..... *Now*' relaxation and sleep CD series. These have been part of British Airways well-being In-flight entertainment since 2012. Her child sleep CD was voted 'Top 5 Best Bedtime Buy' by Practical Parenting & Pregnancy magazine.

Having been a mother of three active little minds herself, Anna offers both a practical and psychological insight into the science of sleep. In Twinkle and the Magic Carpet, she has crafted a bedtime story that is both magical and effective at helping your child drift off and enjoy more restful nights.

For more products and audio downloads by Anna Rowe visit:
www.naturalharmonyproductions.com

Printed in Great Britain
by Amazon